PRINCESS SMARTYPANTS
AND THE
MISSING PRINCES

Look out for …

*Princess Smartypants and the
Fairy Geek Mothers*

Babette Cole

PRINCESS SMARTYPANTS

AND THE MISSING PRINCES

Hodder
Children's
Books

A Catalogue record for this book is available from the British Library

ISBN 978-1-444-92978-2

Hodder Children's Books
A division of Hachette Children's Group
Part of Hodder and Stoughton
50 Victoria Embankment, London, EC4Y 0DZ
An Hachette UK company

www.hodderchildrens.co.uk
www.babette-cole.co.uk

For Freya and her daughters,
Tizane, Bethany, Adela and Leah

CONTENTS

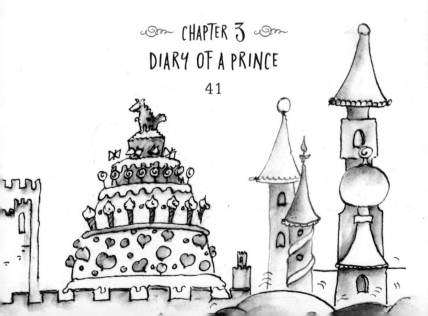

Princess Smartypants is a very unusual princess.

Most princesses wear pretty dresses, lots of make-up and their main mission is to marry a rich handsome prince and live happily ever after.

But Princess Smartypants is very happily *un*married. She is quite content to be a 'Ms' and governs her wacky kingdom of Totaloonia all on her own with huge success – and without the unwelcome help of any dumb princes.

She spends her time looking after her outrageous pets and having lots of fun. She wears dungarees and wellington boots (except when she is riding her trusty motorbike 'Norton' in her leathers). She flies about on her Dragonocodiles and Pollycrocs and has a very naughty pony called Powderpuff.

Princess Smartypants' best friend is her handyman, Eric the Annihilator. He is a very large giant who keeps the castle running and generally takes care of Princess Smartypants.

Although our princess is unusual, that does not mean to say that she is not continually bothered by princes asking for her hand in marriage. After all, she is very pretty and rich. They are always turning up at the castle making a nuisance of themselves, which is a horrible mistake on their part. You see, one kiss from Princess Smartypants will instantly turn them into a

warty toad or slimy frog.

Totaloonia is crawling with princes. They hang out in the castle moat where Eric feeds them on dried flies and locusts. They are actually very happy and well looked after, even though they still dream of finding the right princess to kiss them back into princes again.

Princess Smartypants does understand that most fairytale princesses want to get married. In fact, she has three potential princess friends who are about to get engaged at this very moment in time.

And that is what this story is all about. So let us not waste any more time and get on with this very unusual fairytale.

CHAPTER 1

THE ROYAL
ENGAGEMENT

Princess Smartypants was just polishing the scales on Polly, her Pollyopticus (one of her favourite pets), when the castle doorbell rang.

Eric let down the drawbridge and a pretty coach containing three would-be Princesses clattered into the castle courtyard.

Her friends, Snowy (Snow White), Cindy (Cinderella) and Punzie (Rapunzel), alighted from the carriage and made their way to the

stables where Princess
Smartypants was at work on
Polly. (A Pollyopticus is half
parrot, half octopus, with
a bit of chicken thrown in.)
She removed her heavy-duty
rubber gloves and gave her
friends a big hug. Polly tried
to hug them too but Princess
Smartypants explained to
him that not all young ladies
appreciated this, because
they thought he might eat
them!

They had come to ask
Princess Smartypants a
favour. They were about

to be officially engaged to
the three princes, Charming,
Handsome and Daring, who
had rescued them in their own
Fairytale stories.

Unfortunately, the princes
had very troublesome mothers
who all wanted the official
engagement party to be
held at their own particular
palace. The girls had decided
to take the matter into their
own hands and find an
independent venue.

The trouble was, Punzie
only had a high tower with no
disabled access ...

Cindy just had a kitchen which belonged to her three ugly sisters ...

... and Snowy could only come up with a tiny hut full of very small, bearded gentlemen.

'Hey, Smartypants,' said
Cindy, 'would it be OK if we
had our engagement party at
your castle?'

'It would be the perfect
setting,' added Snowy, 'and it
has disabled access.'

'Also it would stop our future mothers–in-law arguing about where it is going to be held,' said Punzie.

'My dear friends,' said Princess Smartypants, 'I would be delighted to help. Just tell me what theme you want for the party and my court magician, Mervin, will conjure it up in an instant.'

The girls had decided that the theme should be 'Field and Woodland Romance' with a collection afterwards for the 'Totaloonian Field and Woodland Trust'.

'Excellent idea!' agreed Princess Smartypants. 'The castle caterers will put on such a spread your future mothers-in-law will be very impressed.'

They all hugged each other again, although Princess Smartypants had to restrain an over-affectionate Pollycroc, and it was all arranged for next week.

Cindy handed Princess Smartypants the guest list. Everyone from Fairytale Land was invited, except that naughty little witch, Araminta Allspell.

Princess Smartypants confessed she was a bit worried about the blacklisting of Araminta. 'It's asking for trouble,' she said.

'Our mothers-in-law forbid it,' said Snowy. 'Anyway, she is on holiday at the time in the West Hadies so we should be covered.'

'Nevertheless,' said Princess Smartypants, 'you should get the three queens to send an invitation. Otherwise, they are snubbing her and she won't like that at all!'

The girls said they would try to persuade their future mothers-in-law.

'Let's hope they can agree on something,' said Punzie.

They all hugged again and the three happy friends climbed back into the carriage. It clattered over the cobblestones and out over the drawbridge and was gone.

Eric pulled the bridge up again.

'Did you hear that?' said Princess Smartypants.

'We all know Araminta is a tricksy little brat,' replied Eric.

'She only looks about six but
she is really 600 years old and
a very experienced witch. You
don't rub her up the wrong way
if you have any sense.'

They both had a definite feeling trouble was on its way.

CHAPTER 2

PRINCESS SMARTYPANTS ACCUSED

Trouble was indeed brewing.

Araminta Allspell had cancelled her trip to the West Hadies because she expected an invitation to the royal engagement party and the weddings!

Word had got round in Fairytale Land that all the invitations had been sent out, but even the day before the engagement party her mailbox was empty.

No pigeon had dropped an invitation down the chimney, no hedgehog had galloped up the garden path with one stuck to its spines.

'Just you wait, you snobby lot,' she smirked, stirring her big black cauldron and adding all sorts of nasty things. 'There may be a party but there isn't going to be any engagement or wedding if I can help it!'

* * *

Back at Castle Totaloonia
the engagement party
preparations were a huge
success, thanks to Mervin.

The courtyard had
been turned into a magical
woodland with singing trees,
sparkling lemonade lakes,
delicious edible flowers that
made you want to kiss people,
and chocolate fountains that
bubbled from crystal ponds.
An orchestra of woodland
animals played romantic tunes
to make it the perfect setting
for the official proposal by

the three princes.

The guests arrived in their hundreds. All were delighted to be announced and received by the mothers-in-law and their intended daughters. The princes were to arrive once everyone was assembled with special surprises for their princesses and, of course, the rings.

Everyone stood waiting for them in the courtyard by the strawberry meringue valentine heart trees and the band struck up with 'I Just Called to Say I Love You' to announce the entrance of the three princes.

But there were no princes to be seen!

The band struck up again.

It played the music seven
times, but no royal carriages
or white chargers approached
the castle.

Where were they? Had they
got the right time? Had they
got the right day?

The crowd of guests was
getting uneasy.

Snowy, Cindy and Punzie went bright red with fury.

Was there going to *be* an engagement party or indeed a wedding? Were they being jilted?

'This is disgraceful,' said Grumpy, one of Snowy's bearded little gentlemen. 'How *dare* that idiot, Prince Handsome, treat our lovely Snowy like this!'

'Prince Charming has probably found a better-looking girlfriend with prospects,' laughed Cindy's ugliest sister, pointing at her.

'He could do a lot better than that little floor scrubber!'

'Prince Daring has no idea how much work I have put into Punzie's hair today!' sobbed Antonio La Curler, the hairdresser. 'It has taken me

a week to get it into a bun so no one trips on it and has an accident! He needs a kick up the short back and sides!'

'It's all her fault,' accused Queen Charming, pointing at Princess Smartypants in a very *un*charming way. 'She is well-known for kissing princes and turning them into toads! I would not be surprised if she's toaded our sons and they are in the mote with the rest of her ex-suitors!'

'She's right!' added Queen Handsome. 'I caught sight of the poor things as we passed

over the drawbridge. I am
sure one of them had my son's
eyes!'

This was too much for
Cindy, Punzie and Snowy, who
all fainted like a pack of cards!

The guests mumbled
discontentedly. Led by the
angry mothers-in-law they
advanced towards Princess
Smartypants, forcing her to
back up to the castle wall.

But thank goodness for
Eric! He reached over the
battlements and picked her up
in his giant hand.

'Now, look here,' said

Princess Smartypants,
straightening her tiara from
the safety of Eric's thumb.
'There is no way I could have
toaded your sons because I
have never met them. It is
quite clear that this is the work
of Araminta Allspell because
you silly queens did not
send her an invitation to this
do. I promise I will find the
missing princes. I don't want
Snowy, Cindy and Punzie to be
disappointed. I will get them
to the church on time for their
wedding!'

'You'd better stick to that,

you little toader,' screamed
Queen Charming, 'or we will
have your head off! You have
seven days before the wedding
so get busy!'

With that, she turned and
marched out of the castle
followed by the two other
queens and their guests.

'Well, that was grateful of
them,' said Eric as the guests'
coaches, air balloons, flying
machines and steamrollers
disappeared over the horizon.

Mervin was furious. 'After
all I've done conjuring up this
lot and then they accuse you of

toading their wretched sons!'
He waved his hand and the
castle courtyard returned to
normal.

Princess Smartypants
sighed. 'Araminta is definitely
behind this and she is never
going to tell us what she has
done with the princes. We'll
just have to look for clues.'

'Apparently, they were last seen yesterday at the Hotel Totaloonia Tropicana,' said the giant.

'Well, that's our first port of call,' said Princess Smartypants. 'Eric, come on.'

CHAPTER 3

DIARY OF A PRINCE

The hotel occupied its own island out in Crazy Sound, about five sea miles off the coast of Totaloonia. So the next day, the giant picked Princess Smartypants up and waded across the lagoon.

Giants' parents usually abandon their babies as soon as they can walk because they are a bit dangerous so Eric had been brought up by wolves in the forests of Totaloonia. Because of this he had developed a good sense of smell. He could sniff out a prince for miles, especially if it had not changed its socks for a while.

As soon as he strode through the surf up on to the beach, his nose started twitching.

'They've definitely been here,' he said, 'but where they are now is anyone's guess. Let's go and ask at the hotel.'

The hotel had a fizzy sea-pop bar where you could lie around on inflatables while mermaids swam about taking your orders.

Princess Smartypants
dissuaded Eric from getting
into the pool. Even one of his
feet would have caused it to
overflow!

Henrietta Hake, one of
the mermaids, swam over
to ask what they would like.
Princess Smartypants ordered
a cockleshell cocktail and Eric
said he would like a whole

barrel of beer-ade. Several
mermaids propelled this over
to him using their tails like
outboard engines.

'Have any of you girls seen
three princes recently?' asked
Princess Smartypants.

'They were here the day
before yesterday,' said Sandy
Eel. 'We were serving them
buttered toast here in the

pool. I remember because they complained it was not as good as their mothers'.'

'Then they went down to the beach for a swim,' said Celia Shrimpnet. 'We did not see them after that.'

'I saw three silly elves frolicking along the shore line beachcombing,' said Misty Spell, 'but I don't know if they had anything to do with it.'

Princess Smartypants and Eric thanked the mermaids for their help.

They decided to go down to the beach to look for evidence.

'What's that over there by that palm tree?' said Princess Smartypants.

Eric strode on through the sand and stopped at a pile of discarded princely clothing including crowns, swords, boots, spurs and smelly socks.

'**POO!**' exclaimed Princess Smartypants as she lifted up a sock with the Charming coat of arms embroidered on it. There were some spurs with an engraving on the inside thread: '*To my Darling Daring, love from Mummy.*'

Princess Smartypants rifled through the pockets of a purple tunic trimmed with ermine. She pulled out a diary which obviously belonged to Prince Handsome. The entry from two days ago made interesting reading ...

5 April

Today has brought shocking news!

My two friends, Charming and Daring and I decided to have a picnic on the beach before our big Engagement Party tomorrow at Castle Totaloonia.

A really scruffy crow flew over and told us that the whole engagement and wedding was off because our future brides had been kidnapped by a smelly troll and held to ransom!

As we could not possibly afford the huge sum, it suggested we disguise ourselves as elves and rob the Royal Bank of Totaloonia. We have to give the money to Araminta Allspell and she will tell us where to find this revolting troll and rescue our fianceés!

Luckily three elves came wandering along the beach so we nabbed them and pinched their clothes. We've gone to rob the bank!

Princess Smartypants dialled the manager of the bank on her mobile phone. Sure enough, it had been robbed yesterday by three elves!

'That troll has got to be Obnox Pong,' said Eric. 'He is the nastiest and smelliest troll in Fairytale Land. He is so terrible that no one goes near him. Poor girls, being kidnapped by him! And those princes don't stand a chance. I don't know where Obnox lives but he will be building a bridge somewhere, because that is what trolls do.'

'Can you sniff him out?' asked Princess Smartypants.

'Yes,' said Eric, 'but it may be a long way so let's wait until morning.'

CHAPTER 4

THE RIVER TROLLS

As soon as the sun was up, Princess Smartypants climbed into Eric's hand and he followed his nose toward the distant kingdom of Fairytale Land.

As he waded he caused a wake, much to the amusement of the Dolliepods who swam by his side and played in the foam.

They travelled all day and night, passing other islands, some of which moved on their sea legs to let him go by.

The next day, Eric waded past a shoal of

giant Whalesquids. He was pleased to see his old friend, Tenticallis Blubberworth, leading the others.

'Where are you going, Eric?' he asked, curious to see the giant so far out in the ocean.

'Got to find Obnox Pong,' said Eric. 'He's got three wannabe princesses. Have you seen him?'

'Not for ages,' replied the Whalesquid, 'but he will be building a bridge across a river somewhere. Follow the estuary of the River Rumble and once

you get to Fairytale Land you may find him or some river trolls. They may know where he is.'

Eric and Princess Smartypants thanked the sea creature and waded on.

Fairytale Land eventually came into view, pink and violet in the setting sun.

The estuary emerged to the
north, so Eric changed course,
picking off pink jelly estuary
eels that were sucking at his
knees.

It began to get dark, so
Princess Smartypants climbed
up into Eric's warm hair
and fell asleep.

* * *

Eric woke the princess up at daybreak. He was pointing at some huge footprints in the mud at the side of the riverbank.

'Trolls,' he said, sniffing the air.

At that moment a huge boulder whizzed past his ear and splashed into the water!

It was followed by several more, accompanied by screams and jeers from a troop of river trolls who were hurling them down at him from the mountains above.

Eric had had enough. He caught the next boulder and threw it back with such force that it hit one of the trolls, sending it tumbling into the river.

Trolls do not like getting wet. They never wash, which is why they are always building bridges to avoid stepping in water. They cannot

swim, either, so the troll was
having a horrible time trying
to get out of the river.

'If only we had some soap,'
laughed Princess Smartypants.

'Good idea,' said Eric,
reaching under the water and
grabbing some Spongesoapers.
(These creatures give off a
soapy foam like washing-up

liquid when they are plucked from the rocks where they grow.)

The other trolls ran away when they saw the soap. So Eric grabbed the escaping troll by the hump on the back of its neck.

'If you don't want a good scrub,' he laughed, holding up the Spongesoaper to within an inch of its nose, 'tell me where I can find Obnox Pong.'

The troll went blue, then purple. 'Please don't wash me Eric!' it snivelled. Its bulging red eyes centred on the soapy mass the giant was holding in

his other hand. 'I'll tell you –
I'll tell you – he's building a
bridge over a branch of this
river near Castle Creep. It's
not far!'

Eric dragged the soggy troll
through the water and let it
go on the riverbank. He gave
it a hefty kick on the bottom
to send it on its way, and they
continued theirs.

CHAPTER 5

A
GIANT
BARGAIN

Eric and Princess Smartypants continued up the river as far as Castle Creep. Here the giant stopped and sniffed the air.

'*Ugh!*' he exclaimed. 'Those poor girls having to put up with Obnox's pong. One thing puzzles me, though. Trolls need strong people to help build their bridges. He would hardly kidnap potential princesses to do this because they would be as weak as three blind mice.'

Princess Smartypants thought for a moment. She

pulled out her mobile phone
and dialled Cindy's number.
Cindy revealed she was in
the kitchen,
scrubbing
the floor!

Punzie was at the
hairdressers ...

... and
Snowy
had taken her
oldest tiny bloke,
Sleepy, to the
chiropodist.

'I've got it!' Princess Smartypants announced.

'It's just a trick! The girls are all safely at home! Araminta has *lied* to the three princes. She has told them that Obnox has their fiancées so that they'll search him out and rescue them. In fact, it's the *princes* Obnox has as prisoners. He wants them as slaves to build his bridges. Those silly boys should have checked with the girls before they went off on the rescue!'

'You are right!' said Eric, 'but how are we going to get

Obnox to part with them?'

'Ha, ha!' said Princess Smartypants. 'I have a plan! All we need is a long piece of rope ...' She whispered the rest of her instructions into his huge ear.

Eric found a rope attached to a disused barge on the jetty at Castle Creep.

'Fantastic,' said Princess Smartypants. 'Now, tie one end around your neck, give me the other – and follow me.'

It was a strange sight to see a tiny princess leading an enormous giant on a rope as they plodded towards Obnox's bridge. The pong grew worse and worse but they had to carry on.

As they rounded the river, the bridge came into sight. Obnox was shouting orders at three sorry-looking elves who were straining to move a huge tree trunk.

Princess Smartypants
pretended to drag Eric up to
the edge of the bridge.

'Excuse me, Mr Troll,' she
shouted, holding her nose
between her finger and thumb.

Obnox Pong turned and his
eyes nearly popped out of their
sockets.

'I have heard you have some puny elves working for you,' continued our clever princess. 'I wondered if I could make a bargain with you? I need help with my garden and this big stupid giant here is no good for the job. He keeps standing on my daffodils. What I want are three nice little garden elves. My giant would be far more useful to you for building your bridges, so I was wondering if we could do a swap?'

Obnox Pong could not believe his luck. 'Send it over

then!' he bawled.

'Elves first, please,' returned Princess Smartypants.

Obnox thought for a bit. Was this some kind of trick? However, he could not resist the thought of owning Eric – and what could this little princess do to him?

'All right,' he agreed, pushing the three elves forward, 'but when they reach your side send the giant to me.'

'Right you are,' said Princess Smartypants, giving the rope a tug.

Obnox let the elves go and they stumbled over the bridge towards Smartypants and Eric. As they approached she recognised the elves as the missing princes from their photos in *Fairytales Today* magazine but showed no reaction as they joined her at her end of the bridge.

'Let me have it then,' shouted Obnox, standing on the opposite side, waiting for his bargained giant.

'With pleasure,' shouted Princess Smartypants.

Eric stamped so hard on

their side of the bridge it catapulted up like a seesaw.

With a terrible roar up went Obnox Pong high into the sky and away over the mountains. Never to be seen again!

Eric laughed so hard he caused an avalanche, which hopefully buried the smell.

The elf princes and Princess Smartypants all shouted, **'YES,'** and high fived.

Eric swung them all up onto his shoulder and headed for home.

'But first, it's time we paid a visit to Araminta Allspell,' said Princess Smartypants.

So Eric strode along the river until he found the village where she lived.

CHAPTER 6

A
WITCH
DIS-SPELLED

Araminta Allspell was sitting in her den cackling as she counted out all the bank's money she had forced the princes to steal for her. Calliper, her familiar crow, sat preening his feathers on her shoulder.

'The fools,' she giggled, 'if only they knew their intended brides have been safe and sound at home all this time. Those stupid boys are in captivity with Obnox Pong for ever and there will be no beastly wedding. It serves them right for not inviting me.'

Just then, there was a loud pounding on her door that made her jump, and Calliper fell off her shoulder with a squawk.

Before she could scoot up the chimney a giant foot

kicked her door in to reveal
Princess Smartypants, three
princes in elf gear and Eric's
feet.

No one looked more
shocked than Araminta!

She pointed at Smartypants and hissed, 'I'll teach you to trick me. A pair of knickers you shall be!'

But oh dear! Instead of a bolt of blue lightning emitting from her finger it only smouldered like a candle and went out! Princess Smartypants did not turn into the pair of frilly undies as Araminta had intended!

The little witch knew full well that by rescuing the princes, Princess Smartypants had broken her spell and her magic was severely disabled.

Princess Smartypants and
the princes marched in over
the broken door.

'Now then, Araminta,' said
Princess Smartypants. 'Give all
that money back to the bank, or
Eric here will eat you up. And
there is no use trying to magic
your way out of it because you
are dis-spelled.'

'It's *my* money,' whined
Araminta, 'I've been saving it
up out of my pocket money for
600 years.'

'No, it isn't,' said Princess
Smartypants, holding a note
up to the light. 'This has my

recent portrait on it and I was not alive 600 years ago!'

'Hand it over, Araminta,' said Eric, lying down so he could look through the window. 'I am very hungry and witch is my favourite snack.' He licked his lips.

That was too much for Araminta! She gave in and let the princes stuff all the money into shopping bags.

'This would not have happened if your snobby mothers hadn't excluded me from your wedding,' she sulked.

'If you promise to behave yourself I will see that you get your invitation,' said Princess Smartypants.

They left her to mull that over and phoned the bank manager to explain what had happened. She told him she had found the money and was bringing it back.

* * *

The village clock struck
midday.

'Oh my giddy aunt!' said
Princess Smartypants. 'We
have only two days to get you
guys back to Totaloonia for the
wedding and there's lots still
to do yet!'

CHAPTER 7

TO THE ROYAL WEDDINGS

Eric sped back to Totaloonia, carrying Princess Smartypants and the princes as quickly as he could. In fact, he waded at such speed he left a wake behind him like a battleship.

The wedding ceremonies were happening very soon and Princess Smartypants had to lock the frogs up in the dungeons. There was no way they were getting out to cause havoc. It was much too risky as so many princesses would be there for them to kiss!

They passed the gorge

where the river trolls had
attacked, but they all scuttled
off when they saw Eric.

At the mouth of the estuary
he turned out to sea. This time,
the moveable islands had to
shift pretty quickly to make way
for him.

'I see you got your princes,' yelled Tenticallis Blubberworth as the shoal of Whalesquids swam by.

'Thanks to you, mate,' shouted Eric, waving a huge hand goodbye.

Darkness fell and Eric waded on
in the moonlight. The princes
were sitting next to Princess
Smartypants on his left shoulder,
hanging on to his braces.

'How much longer before
we reach land?' whined Prince
Charming. 'I'm getting hungry
and I'm missing *Top Carriage*,
my favourite TV programme.

Mummy would have arranged a delicious TV dinner and had it brought on a tray. I hope Cindy does it as well as Mummy, and that she doesn't want to watch *her* favourite programme on *another* channel.'

'I'm cold,' shivered Prince Handsome. 'Mummy would have warmed my socks and pyjamas by now. I hope Snowy knows what temperature I like.'

'I'm looking forward to marrying Punzie,' said Prince Daring, 'but I hope her hair is not going to be a nuisance. It was OK to climb up when I

rescued her but she spends
so long at the hairdresser I'm
going to get huge hairy bills!'

Princess Smartypants
had to restrain herself from
'toading' them all right
there and then. Instead, she
snuggled into Eric's hair and
thought how lucky she was
not being married to some
whingeing prince.

Eric powered on through
the water until dawn broke on
the morning of the wedding.
Totaloonia could be seen on
the horizon and he broke into
a splashing run. Everybody

held on tight to his braces
straps as he sped along like a
powerboat.

***

Once on dry land, the first
stop was the bank to return
the money. The second was
the Hoodies' Cloak Shop at
the end of the street. Princess
Smartypants had a plan to get
her own back on the princes'
pesky mothers. They had
been leaving menacing text
messages on her phone like:
'Get my son to the church by
midday, Smartypants, or you
are TOAST!'

She quickly sent them return texts saying: 'Get a wedding invitation to Aramina Allspell immediately or I will not deliver them to the church at all!'

* * *

The castle clock stuck midday
and Totaloonia Cathedral
looked splendid. All was ready
for the weddings. The pews
were packed with guests on
either side. The mothers-in-
law were most fed up because
the front one was taken up
entirely by Snowy's seven
little friends.

Once the guests were all
settled, Princess Smartypants
and three hooded figures made
their way up to the alter rail. The
mothers-in-law and the guest
mumbled in a suspicious way.

The hedgehog band struck
up with 'Here Comes the
Bride' and to everyone's

surprise Araminta Allspell
skipped up the isle in her
flower girl outfit, spreading
rose petals in front of Snowy
on Happy's arm, Punzie on
Antonio's and Cindy on her
eldest ugly sister's!

The escorts left the girls at the altar rail, where three hooded figures were waiting for them. Princess Smartypants gave the nod and the hooded cloaks were thrown aside, revealing three elves!

The mothers-in-law went crazy.

'Stop this wedding at once!' shouted Queen Charming leading the other two queens up the aisle.

'Off with that minx's head!' shouted Queen Handsome.

'Where are our boys?' howled Queen Daring.

The three elves turned round.

'Hello, Mummy,' they all said at once, and everybody burst out laughing.

The queens were returned to their pews and the ceremony proceeded.

Princess Smartypants had the job of being best girl and handed over the rings. After that, the three couples were declared Prince and Princess, man and wife.

The mothers-in-law all cried and Araminta danced back down the aisle, spreading

more rose petals. She led the
happy couples out into the
sunshine.

Everyone cheered like
mad. Eric was waiting outside
with a squadron of Pollycrocs
who performed a spectacular
fly-past. They puffed red
smoke out into the sky which

read, 'We wish you a Long and Happy Love.' Another squadron sped past puffing out rainbow-coloured smoke, saying, 'Thanks to Princess Smartypants!' And a further one went past saying, 'And Eric!'

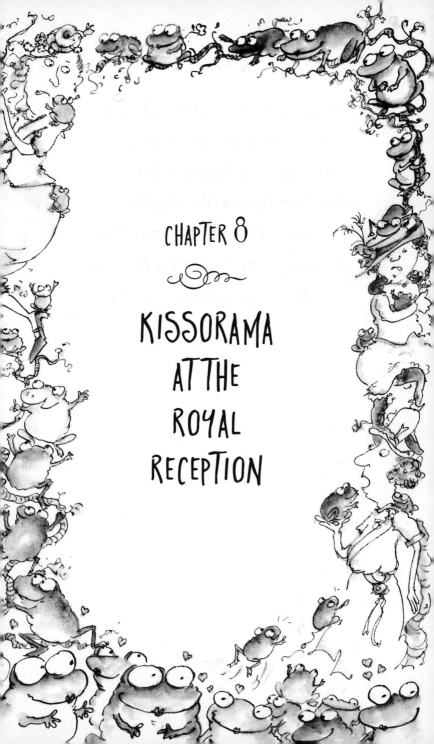

CHAPTER 8

KISSORAMA AT THE ROYAL RECEPTION

Princess Smartypants had arranged that the princes and their new princesses could have their wedding reception at Castle Totaloonia. Mervin had conjured up the perfect fairytale palace on the lawn. Being made of crystal, it put the one in the Disney movies to shame.

He had also made an enormous cake about the size of a small tower, and there were wondrous jelly elephants, peacock eggnogs, roasted glitterballs and the most magnificent banquet ever.

Everybody sat down, and it was time to tuck in.

But when it came to the speeches Princess Smartypants, being best girl, had to deliver one with funny stories about the brides.

She remembered the time Punzie used tons of hairspray and was declared a hazard to aircraft by Dragon Airways.

And how Snowy caused a shopping catastrophe by taking Bashful, Doc, Dopey, Happy, Sleepy, Sneezy and Grumpy shopping for wedding suits at Mothercare because

she thought it would be the
only shop with small enough
clothes for them.

And, of course, no one
knew Cindy got terrible
bunions from those glass
slippers.

Everyone laughed.

It was time to cut the cake but it was so tall the happy couples had to be levitated by Mervin to reach it.

Up they went and everyone cheered as the swords were drawn ready to cut the first massive slice. But as they were raised the cake exploded and out hopped hundreds of frogs and toads!

Princess Smartypants' ex-suitors had slithered through the dungeon bars. They had swum the moat and the lake to the fairytale wedding palace where

they had hidden themselves in the cake waiting for the right moment to pounce on as many princesses – or anyone else, really – as possible.

They swarmed over the alarmed guests covering them in slimy kisses in the hope that they might get turned back into princes.

Matrons fainted, princesses swooned. The mothers-in-laws tried to bat them off with their sceptres!

'That's torn it!' said Princess Smartypants. 'ERIC! HELP!'

As the giant was in charge of feeding the frogs and toads he knew just what to do. He saved the day by reaching over the battlements for their feeding tin which he rattled very loudly.

'Come on, lads,' he shouted. 'Dinner time!'

This worked a treat because no frog or toad prince can resist a dried fly or locust. They much prefer them to kissing princesses. They wriggled and hopped over the slippery guests, following Eric towards the mote where he ladled out their favourite food. They guzzled the lot and lay contentedly on the lily pads, burping.

There was a stony silence and everyone looked at Princess Smartypants.

'Well,' she said, 'that's what I call a TOADALLY

perfect wedding day!'

Cindy, Punzie and Snowy giggled, which broke the levitation spell and the happy couples tumbled down into a gigantic green jelly elephant with a resounding **PLOP!**

The whole wedding party howled with laughter. The band started to play a rock 'n' roll tune called 'Let's Go to the Hop' and everyone stared jiving. Even Eric had a go which caused an earthquake over in Fairytale Land and the river trolls fell into the water.

EPILOGUE

The happy couples left in a golden coach drawn by eight white unicorns. Araminta tied a big sign saying 'Just Married' on the back and set off a load of firecrackers. This spooked the unicorns and they shot off into the sky at a mad bolt, reaching the honeymoon destination in record time!

Eric and Smartypants waved goodbye and he carried her back to the castle.

When the guests had all gone Mervin clicked his fingers. All traces of the fairytale wedding vanished and life in Totaloonia went back to usual.

'Well, what an adventure,' said Eric. 'I'll just go and make sure the frogs are all right and then we can have a nice cup of tea by the telly. I have had enough of fairytales.'

But just then the castle doorbell went again and a

rather plump, middle-aged
lady in a crossover pinny
carrying a large hand bag
hurried across the courtyard.

'Hello,' said Princess
Smartypants, 'and what can I
do for you?'

'Smartypants,' said the disgruntled lady. 'You won't remember me because you were a baby at the time but I am Doris Roundbotham, your fairy godmother and I need your help. It is a scandalous story!'

Eric and Smartypants looked at each other and sighed. 'Oh no, not *another* fairytale!' they said together.

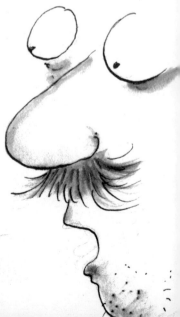